Islington
BOOKSWAP

Please take me home!
(better still, swap me with one of yours!)

Funny stories, sad stories, mystery stories, scary stories, stories about school, stories about friends, stories about animals, stories about family...books full of fascinating facts. If you liked this story book, we've got lots more like it that you can borrow from our libraries!

Join your local Islington Library today!
www.islington.gov.uk/libraries

D1147839

With love to all my family, especially Madeleine,
and with many thanks to Paul Dowswell – LA

For my brother Steven, with love.
Thanks go to my friends at the Lion & Unicorn,
The Pavilion and the lovely people at Scholastic – SH

First published as
Ordinary Oscar in 2008
by Scholastic Children's Books
This edition first published in 2010
by Scholastic Children's Books
Euston House, 24 Eversholt Street
London NW1 1DB
a division of Scholastic Ltd
www.scholastic.co.uk
London ~ New York ~ Toronto ~ Sydney ~ Auckland
Mexico City ~ New Delhi ~ Hong Kong

PB ISBN 978 1407 11583 2

I WANT TO BE FAMOUS

Laura Adkins & Sam Hearn

SCHOLASTIC

In the **moonlit** garden of 16 Slug Street,
the snails are busy.
Slowly, they **munch** and **crunch**
the tasty, tender leaves of potted plants
and juicy lettuce.
They are all **happy** snails.

Well, **nearly**
all of them....

Oscar Slimeglider
was **not** happy.
"I'm **tired** of sleeping
all day," he said.

"I'm **fed up** with
eating all night.

"I'm **bored** with being greenish-grayish-brownish.

"I want other snails to look at me and say, 'Wow! There's **Oscar Slimeglider!**'

I want to be **different**....

"I want to be FAM!

"Oh, Oscar!"

"Slime my autograph book!"

"Nonsense!" said Oscar's dad. "What's wrong with sleeping all day? What's wrong with eating all night?"

"And what's wrong with being greenish-grayish-brownish?" said Oscar's mom. "Your twenty-five brothers and sisters never complain."

"We never complain!"

But Oscar was
determined.

"The Wise Old Snail
will know what to do,"
he declared.

So off he went.

"What do you want to be famous **for**?" asked the Wise Old Snail.

"Can you paint?

Dance?

Play the guitar?"

Oscar shook his head.

"Being famous isn't **always** easy, you know," said the Wise Old Snail. "Are you **sure** about this?"

Oscar nodded.

"Very well then," said the Wise Old Snail. "You're going to need a bit of **magic**."

And he told Oscar what to do.

Oscar waited patiently for the sun to rise.

Then he **turned** around three times and cried,

"Slime, slime! Slither, slither!

Fairy Godsnail, please come hither!"

The **Fairy Godsnail** appeared. "So you want to be famous?" she asked.

Oscar wiggled eagerly. "Yes, please!"

"There's only one thing to do then," replied the **Fairy Godsnail**. "I shall grant you three wishes. But choose carefully," she warned.

Then she waved her magic wand and disappeared.

Oscar closed his eyes tightly and made a wish....

Slowly, Oscar opened his eyes.
"Look at me!" he gasped.

"I'll be famous for being the most marvellous mollusc!

I'm a stunning, stupendous, spectacular snail! Everyone will admire me."

And sure enough, someone was admiring Oscar...

"BIGGER!"

Oscar landed in town. He was
bigger than a bus, bigger than
six buses glued together.

As the sun began to sink, Oscar slithered
into the woods to hide.

"Now I'm famous for being frightening,"
he said, "and I have no friends."

Oscar began to cry.

"I want to go **home** to Mom and Dad and my twenty-five brothers and sisters. I wish I was just **ordinary** Oscar again."

And just like that...

he was home.

"Where have you been, Oscar?" asked his dad. "We've been awfully worried about you."

"We thought you might have been squashed!" said his mom.

"Now, it's dinnertime," she said. "I've got some **tasty**, tender leaves, just for you."

"Mmm, my favorite," said Oscar. "Maybe being **ordinary** isn't so bad after all."

But sometimes, just sometimes, even an **ordinary** snail can do **extraordinary** things.

Six weeks later…

Daily

THAT'S MY BOY

By **Mike Mollusk**
Garden Correspondent

Shellebrity: Oscar Slimeglider rescues Mom trapped in shifting s

CONTEST: Win a copy of

Snail

www.dailysnail.sl.ime

70 Leaves

When Mrs. Gertrude Slimeglider fell into some shifting soil, she was overcome by panic.

Gertrude, who is expecting sixty eggs next week, was trapped.

Meanwhile, her twenty-six children—Agnes, Bernard, Cornelius, Destiny, Electra, Fifi, Georgina, Heathcliff, Ingrid, Jethro, Keanu, Lavender, Mozart, Norbert, Oscar, Pandora, Quentin, Rupert, Sigmund, Thomas, Ursula, Veronica, Wilma, Xavier, Yeats, and Zebedee— roamed the flower bed.

"I told Agnes to get her dad, but because he was so far away I knew that would take a long time," she said.

With her husband on the other side of the garden, Gertrude was desperate, until clever Oscar came to the rescue.

"Oscar is a brave and caring snail."

Oscar, a Saint Mollusk pupil, gathered his siblings together. Under his direction, they began to eat the surrounding plants. The courageous youngster kept his cool and soon the soil began to shift, allowing Gertrude to escape.

"Oscar is a brave and caring snail. I'm really proud of him," said Gertrude. "When my husband gets home and hears about what happened, I know he'll be proud, too."

The End